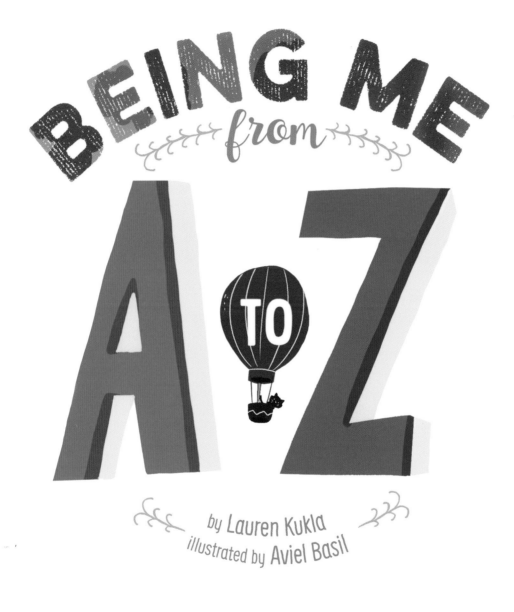

BEING ME from A TO Z

by Lauren Kukla

illustrated by Aviel Basil

A is for **adventure**,
to fearlessly roam
and see awesome places
so far from your home.

B is for brave

when you start feeling small.
Be bold, you are brilliant,
so hold your head tall.

C stands for **caring**,
but you'll need courage, too,
to show compassion for those
who are different from you.

ADOPT A PET

D is for **daring**
to do a great deed
that shows that you care
about someone in need.

E is for **empathy**—you'll be especially wise
if you experience life through another kid's eyes.

F is for **friendship**—
finding someone who's true
and who opens your mind
to new points of view.

G is for **grateful**,
the grace to be glad
for all of the good things you
have and you've had.

H stands for **helping** and doing your part. Lending a hand makes a happy heart.

I is for **imagine**,
the ideas you'll find,
when you invite the
improbable into your mind.
Incredible inventions are
just a daydream away,
so let your thoughts wander
and let your brain play.

J is for **justice**
and doing what's right,
a job that's not easy,
but still worth the fight.

K is for **kindness**,
the goodness you share,
which sometimes means doing
much more than what's fair.

L is for **love**

that you'll get and you'll give
if you let your heart lead you
as long as you live.

Loving others feels lovely,
it's a grand thing to do,
but it's important to learn
how to love yourself too.

M is for **mistakes**—
yes, make them you will,

misssteps and missed
chances and milk
that you spill.

You'll hurt someone's feelings, you'll step on a toe.

Make every mistake a new mission to grow.

N stands for **nature**,
from newt to narwhal,
all your animal neighbors,
both big and small.
They need you to care
for the planet we share
and clean up its forests
and oceans and air.

O is for **outrageous**,
so open your brain
to outlandish opinions it can
barely contain.

P is for **persistence**

to chase down big dreams
and perseverance to realize
impossible schemes.

Q stands for **questions**—
ask one thousand and four.
In your quest for the answers,
you'll ask even more!

R is for **resilience**
when those answers surprise.
You've learned something
new! Now rethink and revise.

S is for setback.
You'll have quite a few.

Sometimes sad things will happen to you.

T is for **trusting** a friend when life's tough. Just talking about it can help you through stuff.

U is for **unique**—
it takes guts to be proud
and to be yourself
in the midst of a crowd.

V stands for **volume**.
When something's not right,
raise your voice and speak out
with all of your might!

PROTECT
WILDLIFE!

W is for **wonder**—
what, why, where, and how.
The world's out there waiting
to make you say, "Wow!"

X is for **excitement**,
you'll have so much more
if you experiment, examine,
expand, and explore.

Y is for **yeah**, **yippee**, and **yahoo**!

Z stands for one in a **zillion**—

that's YOU!

Let these ABCs guide you
in making each day
a story you're proud of in every way.
With the words that you say
and the things that you do,
the world is so lucky to have
someone like you!

Published in 2019 by Beaming Books, an imprint of 1517 Media. All rights reserved. No part of this book may be reproduced without the written permission of the publisher. Email copyright@1517.media.
Printed in the United States of America.

25 24 23 22 21 20 19   1 2 3 4 5 6 7 8
ISBN: 978-1-5064-5259-3

Written by Lauren Kukla
Illustrated by Aviel Basil
Art Direction by Aruna Rangarajan
Design and Production by Mighty Media, Inc.

Names: Kukla, Lauren, author. | Basil, Aviel, illustrator.
Title: Being me from A to Z / written by Lauren Kukla ; illustrated by Aviel Basil.
Description: Minneapolis, MN : Beaming Books, 2019. | Summary: "From Awesome Adventures to being one in a Zillion, each letter of the alphabet inspires kids to be their best selves in Being Me from A to Z"-- Provided by publisher.
Identifiers: LCCN 2019005693 | ISBN 9781506452593 (hardcover : alk. paper)
Subjects: | CYAC: Stories in rhyme. | Conduct of life--Fiction. | Alphabet.
Classification: LCC PZ8.3.K9448 Bei 2019 | DDC [Fic]--dc23
LC record available at https://lccn.loc.gov/2019005693

VN0004589;9781506452593;JUN2019

Beaming Books
510 Marquette Avenue
Minneapolis, MN 55402
Beamingbooks.com